Collections

E.H.

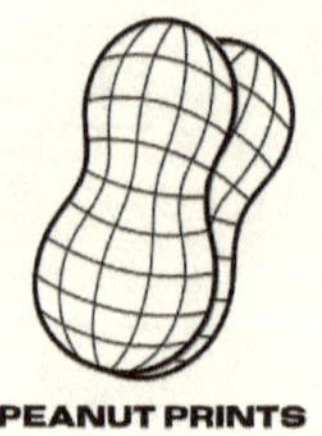
PEANUT PRINTS

Lands of old what secrets do you keep?
Below the wandering hills and beneath the
murky creek,
For many years life has seemed to grow,
But from when or how none ever know,
Is the secret too grand or too simple for us
to see?
Is there no secret at all, and we are all
simply meant to be?
I think not,
Not a stone is unturned without its reason,
And life evolves and changes just like the
seasons,
One day I hope that we evolve enough to
see,
And when we do I hope we still have the
grace to simply be.

The Little Village On the Hill

Beyond the great rivers and streams of the Western Plains, and out of sight from the major cities of man there was a small village atop a hill. It had been there for generations. Generation after generation lessons were passed down from fathers to sons, mothers to daughters, and over the years the little village hadn't changed at all. The lessons had never changed, and it was as if the same people had been living there forever. There are many pathways and windy roads that lead us through life, but for the children of this quiet little village, their paths had already been foretold.

This was not a sad affair, in fact, it was an affair of happy ignorance. Never, in the entire history of the little village had anybody ever asked 'Why'. There was no

'Why' to things, there were only 'How's'. The Farmers knew how to plant the seeds, but not why they grew, and each day of growth was another blessing in their eyes. Sometimes men visited from the great metropolis that spanned throughout the outer world with dreams of progression and evolution for the little village. But, their plans were never understood. The men from the cities used words forged from the bellies of combustion engines that confused and confounded the people of the village, who only spoke the calm language of nature. They knew the language of birds, from the earliest dawn, and the settling dusk. They knew the language of the rivers, that flowed and brought balance throughout the land. Of the trees that swayed together as one in the wind, and caressed the face of the farmers that worked the land. They had no use for the engines that clogged the air and polluted the rivers, or the combustion vehicles of the great cities. They rode atop wagons pulled by horse, as their parents had done before them. They had no use for harvester machines, for they worked the land with their hands alone, and to rob them of their purpose was to rob them from their heritage. The men of the cities tried, but failed, and soon their vehicles no longer grinded and gnashed their way up to the village on the hill.

Many years have passed since the day I visited that village atop the hill. I have watched the cities rise to the heavens, but they have risen too tall. Too tall even for the great sun, whose light is blocked out by the impenetrable walls of their progression. Now the cities lie beneath the great shadows that are cast by themselves.

In my old age, I dream of that village atop the hill. The soft sounds of trickling rivers, flowing through the farms. The collective awakening of birds that fill the morning air with music, and lull it to sleep in the evenings. I dream of the air, and the sun. I'm too old to make the journey back now. But I know that the village is just the same as it always has been, and that is what brings me peace.

A Stroke of Luck

The sound of lasers and cannons ripped through the air of the dingy country pub. The local boys from the Dairy Plant had knocked off early and couldn't wait another hour before slapping their paycheques through a couple of their favourite pokie machines.

"This one's ready to pop," said Bill, an old timer whose skin was worn and leathery from hard years working beneath the sun.

"You say that 'bout every fuckin' machine you sit at," replied Dave as he lowered a freshly poured schooner from his lips. He licked the froth away from the stubble beneath his nose.

"When's the last time you fuckin' won anythin' on this fuckin' machine anyway?" he added as he sat down.

"Fuck off cunt," started Bill, "I've won fuckin' heaps."

Bill leant over on his seat and pulled his wallet from his work pants, sifting through old receipts and tickets, he found a scrunched up twenty dollar note and tried to flatten it out.

Dave sat down next to Bill and did the same. "Managements doin' my fuckin' head in. Bunch of fuckin' paper pushers couldn't undo a fuckin' bolt if their ball sacks were stuck in it," said Bill as he slipped his twenty into the machine.

The Machine lit up with sounds and explosions and Bill began tapping away.

"Watch me get a feature cunt..." he said under his breath as he stared transfixed at the screen.

He slapped the betting button twice with the maximum amount of money he could bet. He had done this many times before. So often that he felt a yearning for the dingy room with the stained carpet, that stank of stale smoke and spilt beer, and on long days on the job he often caught himself day dreaming about the room.

Suddenly, a dancing Mexican jumped out onto the screen and yelled "More Chilli!", illuminating the creases and folds Bills worn out face.

Bill lowered his schooner from his lips, this time was different, the music was grander, and as the Mexican shot his guns and danced the sign atop the machine flashed 'Mega Pay'.

Bill's mouth opened silently as he watched the money tally up on the screen. Thirty thousand dollars' worth.

Dave roared in excitement next to him, "You're fuckin' jokin'!" Bill shook his head in disbelief. "You fuckin' won!" Dave roared again, launching himself from out of his chair and clasping Bill tightly on the shoulders.

All of Bill wanted to keep betting, but he knew that this was the greatest win he'd ever get, and with effort he removed the winning ticket from the machine.

Still in disbelief he and Dave walked over to the cashier.

The cashier was a larger man with a short, clean beard and rolled-up sleeves that revealed tattooed-covered arms.

He paused when he looked at the ticket that Bill had given to him, but after a moment he smiled.

"Congratulations mate," he said, before disappearing to the back room and returning with a small bag filled with notes.

Bill took the bag silently and looked in.

He removed a one hundred dollar bill and gave it to Dave, "Beers on me tonight." And he turned to leave the pub.

"Where you goin'?" Dave asked.

"Gotta go show Shaz, she'll be over the moon," replied Bill.

Bill got in his car and made his way home, driving through windy hills and bumpy dirt roads long since forgotten by the local council. Half an hour passed before he arrived in front of an old, slanted looking house. He climbed the wooden steps onto the porch and walked through the door.

He found his wife Shaz lying in bed, she had been there for some time, overcome by immunity-related illnesses.

"How was work?" she said as Bill dropped his keys onto the table. He didn't reply.

"Bill?" she asked again.

He walked over and sat down next to her, "I think we can afford the treatment now."

The next day Bill and Shaz drove two hours to the nearest hospital, and as he drove Bill thought of the dingy room and the flashing machines, and of his friend Dave. He smiled.

He didn't go back to work that week.

Warm Memories

Deep in the Andule Forests at the base of Plume Mountain, there was a dog that roamed the land. His name was Mika, but years before he had been separated from the humans that raised him and he had never heard that name since.
Mika had been owned by an elderly couple who lived in a small cottage on the outskirts of the Forest. Even as a pup he had always stared longingly out into the forests as he dozed on the porch, dreaming of a day where he could roam the world. He dreamt of rushing rivers and rolling hills, and of trees that swayed lazily in the wind. But, his owners were old and had long since passed the days of adventuring, and instead, they sat with him by the fire or tended to their gardens in a state of silent reflection that only comes with age.
The elderly couple loved Mika, and he loved them dearly too, and every night as he

lay next to the cosy fire he fought a losing battle to stay awake.

But, as years passed and Mika grew older he became more and more restless, bound to the small stretch of land behind the fence of the property that made the sight of the forest even more maddening.

One day, when the air was hot and wet, Mika sensed a storm was brewing in the wind. The air was heavy and all that were in tune with nature's movements were silenced in the awe of what they knew would come. The storm was unlike any other. It tore through houses and ripped up farms, and amid the chaos, Mika fled wildly through a newly broken hole in the fence and disappeared into the forest.

He raced through the trees that whipped and cracked in the wind, but his race was not one of joy or excitement at being free, it was one of unbound fear. He was terrified of the howling wind and the trees that bent wretchedly in the storm, of the rain that rushed down from the heavens and made the ground muddy and cold. He lost control of himself, running deeper and deeper into the forest until he found a cave. He whimpered in the darkness as he waited for the storm to blow over, thinking of the elderly couple back at the cottage, sitting next to the cosy fire.

Finally, the storm passed, and a great beam of sunlight erupted through the clouds. The forest became normal again, the trees swayed back and forth gently, and a rainbow arched itself across the sky as light droplets of rain flecked off of the tree leaves in the forest below.

Mika left his cave, but he was lost. For so long he had run in his uncontrolled state of fear that he had forgotten the way home, and after hours of roaming, he had only found himself deeper in the clutches of the great Andule Forest.

He was scared.

Years passed, although Mika had no sense of time as we see it. He still roamed the forest; however, he had changed. He was no longer scared of the storms when they came, or the howling wind when it blew trees out of their roots. He understood that the land around him had different moods, just as his owners had had. He understood the rushing rivers that held fish beneath their waters, and where to find the deep burrows and caves that he slept in to keep warm. He knew of the other animals, the bears and wolves too. He knew of the rolling hills and dense woods, waterfalls, and mountains. The Forest had become his home, just as he had always dreamt, and he was happy.

But sometimes, when storms came he still dreamt that he was back inside the house with the old couple, sitting lazily by a cosy fire.

Constant Erosion

Along the coasts of the South there was a boy that played by the sea. He loved the sounds of crashing waves, and the sight of the wide empty horizon before him.
Every day he climbed to the top of the headland and looked out towards the never-ending stretch of ocean before him, where he let his imagination wonder to lands that were far and wide. But one afternoon the boy had a thought as he watched the waves crash and churn at the base of the headland below. He looked at the fallen rocks, scattered amongst the base of the cliff and realised that little by little the land was falling into the sea. He wondered if one day the ocean would swallow the land completely. He lay awake that night, lost in thoughts of deep sea adventures and fun beneath the crashing waves.
The next day he went straight to his spot on the headland, and watched the waves crash

against the cliff. Every moment there was change. The ocean surged and swirled, and as the great tides pulled the water back they revealed the submerged barnacle-covered boulders that lay like pillars of the world.

He watched the soft breeze change directions, and soon the horizon became choppy and white-capped. There is change in every moment of life. With every new moment, there is a new thought. He wondered if our minds were like the ocean, constantly crashing against the walls of our brains. Would we one day be swallowed entirely by thoughts?

He hoped not.

And just as the boy predicted one day he too changed, and stopped visiting the headland by the sea.

With plans to study he moved inland, and for a time he forgot about the crashing waves and the crumbling rocks that fell newly each day.

It was not until he was much older that he returned, and as he climbed over the rocks he used to fly up as a child he groaned from the aches that come with age. He realised the years had weathered him too. Some of his passions had eroded, aches and pains made him feel more vulnerable, and as he stared down at the crashing waves below he knew that like the rocks he would succumb one day to the world around him and re-join the universal law that everything is only borrowed like a book from the library.

He was old, but with some effort he lay down on the headland and popped his head over the side, and searched for the barnacle covered boulders he used to watch as a child, but they were gone.

Sunset

I was sitting alone at a bus stop in London one night. It was late February and the winter frosts still kept a tight grip. As the wind blew breaths of ice from Siberia my face retreated into the inside of my jacket, leaving just my eyes uncovered and peering at my phone through the darkness. I always thought it was funny how people relate their emotions to the weather. I don't think the weather cares about how you feel. The weather in England is mostly bad, but that point in time was the happiest in my life. I had just moved from Australia with hopes and dreams of making something of myself, and although I was far from that, every day in London held something new and exciting.

I was on a quiet street somewhere in Streatham, and a man approached me from out of the darkness. Being London, my first instinct was that I was probably in for a bad time, but he seemed friendly enough. As he approached me he smiled awkwardly and held his phone out.

"Good Night." He said in a thick accent.

I must have looked at him with a puzzled expression because he immediately stuttered, "English not good…"

We smiled at each other, and after an awkward moment of silence, he began typing on his phone. He finished typing and a robotic voice from his phone said, "Do you know when the bus for Clapham Common comes?"

We both laughed at the strangeness of the situation, and I asked him where he was from so that I could write a response. He said Turkey, so I typed a response in my phone and the same robotic voice relayed my message in Turkish. He beamed as he nodded his head in understanding, and a moment after my bus arrived and I smiled at him before I hopped on.

I climbed to the top level of the bus and stared out of the window when I sat down, but it was night so most of what I saw was just my own reflection, save for the lights of cars, or people walking directly under street lamps. Thinking about that Turkish guy made me wonder how the world managed to operate without phones. The entirety of humanity's teachings and history was accessible at just a touch of a button. There is so much power in phones, but I guess there's not much mystery in anything with them. There were forty or so stops before I had to get off the bus, and as it turned and swayed slowly through the dark side streets of South London I lost myself in thoughts of olden day adventurers getting lost in unknown lands without an idea of where they were, and discovering places they never would have dreamed about. A part of me felt jealous of them. There are no mysteries in my world, and anything that I could ever do or say has already been done and said. There are only a few types of people, and somehow, we all become one of them. So much so that for all my life at that point I had felt like I had met the same people over and over again. That was until the day that I met her.

She blew me away. I thought that I had been in love before, but it felt nothing compared to what I felt when I saw her. Sometimes you cross people in your life that just feel right. Like you were cut from the same stone or something like that. I'm at risk of sounding melodramatic, but she really made my heart skip beats. I moved to London with hopes of making something out of myself, but I never thought that I would end up giving myself away like that.

Every day with her made life seem so beautiful and high. But soon I began to fear the inevitable fall that comes with vertigo. It's the mind's greatest trick to wantonly send you to your demise like that. I remember I'd lose myself to fears and prejudices in my head that had never even happened. I guess when you start thinking like that there's not much that can help you turn back. My fear of losing her quickly turned to jealousy, and soon after our relationship fell to pieces. It wasn't her fault, and it wasn't my fault either, I guess sometimes things just end up like that. The afternoon we broke up was the worst in my life, but I remember the sunset was beautiful.

Memories of The Deep

"Go it you fuck'n pussy!" Taz yelled at his friend Levi as the biggest wave of the day formed in the horizon.

Levi hesitantly eyed the mountain of dark water moving towards them, but he was not one to turn down a challenge from Taz. He swung around on his board and paddled as hard as he could, breathing unsteadily as his heart skipped beats.

The wave picked up before him, and in an instant the entire ocean level had dropped as he stared down over the precipice of the peak.

A moment before he was thrown over the lip he stood up, and as he plummeted down the face of the wave he heard Taz's muffled screech, "YEEEEWWW!"

But something felt wrong from the get go and he knew it, as he collided with the bottom of the wave he felt the nose of his board dip beneath the water, and with a sudden jolt he was flung out into the flats, where the full force of the wave crashed down upon him.

Never before had he taken such a beating from a wave, and as it pushed him deeper it spun and tore at him until he was completely disorientated.

He felt his leg rope snap under the force of the wave, and with it any chance of a quick recovery to the surface.

After what seemed an eternity, the wave let go of him, but he was deep beneath the surface now. He opened his eyes and saw the calm blackness that surrounded him, but what he did not expect to see was someone else staring back. It was a girl, and she was beautiful. Her hair was the colour of the sea, and her skin was soft and dark. She beckoned him towards her, but as much as he wanted to, the need for air was more powerful than the allure of her beauty. He took one last look at her before he kicked and swam as quickly as he could to the surface, gasping for air frantically as he struggled to stay afloat. There were no waves in the horizon, and Taz paddled hurriedly towards him, "Holy shit dude, are you good?"

Levi nodded, still catching his breath, and Taz offered his board. The two held on and kicked themselves to shore. Levi had never been so glad to feel land beneath his feet, and as he clambered up the beach he dropped and rolled over, exhausted.

Taz sat next to him, "Fuck, that would have been mad if you'd made it…"

Levi chuckled as he lay on his back, but suddenly the image of the girl flashed past him.

Any Excuse

The mid-July sun began to set over the dusty country building site where Jonno and his team of apprentice bricklayers had been working all day.

Jonno was digging around the site looking for something, cursing under his breath as he searched before he finally gave up and shouted, "All of ya's line up!" at his apprentices from across the site. At the sound of Jonno's voice, the four apprentices immediately dropped everything and rushed over to where he stood. As they lined up silently they waited uneasily for what was to come. Jonno was clearly in a terrible mood.

"Which one of you little fuckwitt's lost it?" Jonno asked the line of quivering apprentice bricklayers.

He walked back and forth from one end of the line to the other, as a sergeant would do with his soldiers.

One of the braver apprentices cleared his throat but recoiled as Jonno swooped down on him.

"Aye? Did I hear you say something?" he said threateningly to the apprentice.

The apprentice shook his head, "We just don't know what you're talking about?"

Jonno smiled, however, there was no trace of friendliness in his expression. His thirty years of laying bricks out in the sun had only hardened his leathery face, which very rarely showed emotions as it was.

"One of ya's has fuck'n lost my spirit level, and if he doesn't own up to it you're all gonna suffer for it." Jonno barked as he continued to walk up and down the line.

Another apprentice looked as if he was about to speak, and not a moment after Jonno was face to face with him, "Was it you Frankie?"

The apprentice called Frankie shook his head hurriedly, "No… but I just wanted to ask what a spirit level was?"

"Fuck off!" was Jonno's reply.

Jonno stopped, the sun had just dipped beneath the horizon and the first breath of cool dusk air had just swept gently through the building site.

"That's it then." he began, "as of tomorrow none of you get to wear anything but your undies to site."
The entire row of apprentices groaned, and Jonno smiled at their pain.
"Now fuck off home." he finished before he turned and made his way towards his ute.
However, he didn't take three steps before he stopped and dug the end of a dirty spirit level out of the mud.
He looked back at his apprentices and lifted the spirit level above his head, "As you were boys I must have dropped it earlier!"

Changes

There was once an old sandstone tower that stood in the centre of a busy village. Times were different then. Where horse and cart travelled along uneven dirt roads, filled with fruit and vegetables that had been carried from the surrounding villages, all to be sold in the town centre. The sounds of wind rustling through the trees and the songs of birds could be heard all around the sunny little village, and at the turn of every hour the great bells of the tower sounded, and rang across the little village like chimes in the wind.

As time moved on the village changed much, the dirt roads were paved, and the small farms had been pushed further out to the country, replaced by brick houses that lined the cobblestone streets in neatly compacted roads. But the old sandstone tower still stood, and on the turn of every hour the same bells rang and beckoned the townspeople. If one was to stand and observe the town and its people as the bell tolled, he would feel a strange oneness with life. Here were people not only existing, but living out purposes that were individual to them. It's strange how so many people with individual purposes can coexist to create an even greater one together. The sight was a far cry from times not too long before, where man lived from the sweat of his back, and at the mercy of the natural seasons.

The bells tolled, and life was awoken again. But, as time moved on, as it always does, the sound of the great bells was drowned out by the blasts from engines and trains, or the hammers of construction workers that pierced the air crudely as they built skyscrapers around it.

Soon the tower was not a tower at all, it had been dwarfed by the spectres of the skyscrapers that touched the heavens above it.

People no longer stopped to admire the tower and its bells, or the oneness of the little village around them. In fact, people stopped looking around at all, so transfixed they were with where they were going, and soon the tower and its bells were forgotten completely.

Years passed and the tower was no more than an empty shell covered in graffiti. Its windows had been broken and covered in cobwebs.

It became an unsightly thing, and in its old age the bells had rusted upon their hinges, and they could no longer ring.

Eventually the old tower was knocked down, and the memory of it was lost forever. And from out of the rubble a carpark was built in its place.

Kevin's epiphany

Kevin, a thirty-three-year old Marketing Manager has an epiphany.

The greatest feeling I ever had was the day I realised that I was the general public. I used to power walk around the city to work every day, silently cursing slow walkers and zig-zaggers, people on their phones who weren't aware of their surroundings, and most of all people who had no sense of personal space. I despised it, and I despised the general public. In my eyes, they were just a bunch of opened-mouthed sloths, drifting in the breeze from one aimless task to another without so much of a thought of having any goals, or passions, or great loves.

I always felt a sense of pride with myself as I sped walked through the bustling busy streets. I was somebody, and I knew that everyone else could sense it. Just look at the way they all looked at me, every time I looked someone's way I could see they were stealing glimpses at me.

I had passions, goals, and dreams. I loved and had been loved, and in turn, my heart had been broken and I had broken hearts.

But, one day whilst I was standing in line for a Boost Juice, I paused. I was tired that day, and when I lined up behind a queue of several other people I groaned. It was ten o'clock on a Monday, and as I looked at the blank faces of the people in the queue I thought to myself, "what are all these people doing here?"

That's when I realised that I was just people too.

After that day, I looked at people differently, they were just like me.

Madly In love

I never wanted her to know that I loved her. Even though my desire to be with her was so great, there was something poetic about caring from afar, some sweet purity of affairs. But, as secrets always have a way of coming out my love was revealed to her. Not out of my doing, but of Thomas Biles'. You see, from the day I laid my eyes on her I knew instantly that I was in love. I had never felt so full of joy, she was everything I had ever dreamed of.

The only problem was that Thomas Biles was standing by my side, and as I looked over at him I caught the same glimmer in his eyes that I had had. From that day on there was an unspoken rivalry between us. Although we were both physically inept to fight, I felt like a caveman from the stone ages, defending his wife with a club from the other men. We never spoke to one another unless forced to, and one time he even closed the elevator on me.

But there was one thing that I had on him, it was that Elizabeth liked me more, and he knew it.

Every day he'd try and work plans to get Elizabeth to hate me. He tried leaving voicemails on her phone pretending to be me, or he'd write her notes and all of that crazy stuff. It never really worked, my Elizabeth was too smart, and she spotted the inconsistencies between our handwritings in an instant.

"I love you." That's all I wanted to say to her, and then who knows, she could have been mine. But, I never did it, I just knew that I couldn't bear to be without her, and if she didn't feel the same, we would inevitably grow apart. No, it was best to say nothing at all. But one day, after Elizabeth and I had been placed together for a group job, we spent the entire day laughing with one another right in front of Thomas. It was clear to him that I was winning, and so while I was in the bathroom he told her everything. He told her that I loved her, and he also told her that I had been bullying him. She didn't react the way that I thought she would. She looked at me a way that I had never seen her look at me before, and my heart stopped.

"Angus…" she began. I nodded enthusiastically, "Yes, yes," praying that she would fall to her knees and proclaim her undying love for me.
But she shook her head, "Angus… I'm sorry, I have a boyfriend."
I didn't know what to say, I tried to get words out, I tried to tell her that it was all a lie and that Thomas was making it up because he didn't like me very much, but all that came out was splutters.
She smiled pitifully, and left my desk.
I looked at Thomas in disbelief, "What have you done…"
He smiled, "Now we're even."

To be continued…

Ignorance is Bliss

A hundred thousand butterflies fluttered across the base of the mountain. The breeze was warm with summer air, and as it caressed the town below it also pushed the butterflies forward gently.

The townspeople called these times the flower skies, for the thousands of butterflies that floated above them, looked like flowers. No one had ever journeyed to the top of the mountain, and over the years there had been much speculation over the origination of the butterflies. Argath, the town's herbalist, believed that they sprouted out from the earth and trees as gifts of the summer. Montga, the town's priest believed that they came from the heavens themselves. The more you talked to people the more you realised that everyone's opinions differed, but no one was truly sure. Jurk, the apprentice blacksmith was the only person that seemed not to have an opinion at all. And as the townspeople bickered and argued, Jurk tapped away at his anvil merrily.

But soon he even became curious too.

He decided late one evening that the next morning he would pack his things early and journey to the top of the mountain. He would settle it all, and as the sun began to rise dully he hoisted up his rucksack and began his ascent up the titan.

He trudged all morning before finally deciding to rest above a small platform on the mountainside. He looked down at his village below. He had never seen it from this perspective before. They all looked so small to him, and as he cast his eyes over the horizon before he scanned the open lands before him. A river winded through the grassy lands and disappeared into the horizon, and in the very distance he could make out the outline of mountains that looked just the same as his one.

That afternoon, after hours of gruelling climbing he finally reached the peak of the mountain, and to his surprise, it was nothing like he had thought it would be at all. The peak was broken and hollow, and inside, not too far down was a dense forest with bright green leaves. Jurk wiped the sweat from his forehead and made his way down slowly to the edge of the forest.

He peered into the dense trees, and, unsure if his mind was playing tricks on him, he thought he could see a purple light emanating from the heart of the forest. He entered the dense overgrowth, and climbed silently, careful not to attract any attention from unwanted beasts. But he encountered nothing on his path, and as he crept deeper and deeper the purple glow grew stronger.

He finally reached an opening through the forest, he walked through but stopped immediately. The floors were covered in caterpillars. It is worth noting that to you and I a caterpillar is symbolic of inner beauty, we see grace in the way it squirms, knowing that one day they will become butterflies. But to Jurk, who did not understand the nature of caterpillars as we do, they were horrific. Never before had he seen something squirm and writhe about aimlessly on the ground. He couldn't see any butterflies, and, taking one more disgusted look around him he turned his back and climbed down the mountain. The next morning after he had rested the village people swarmed around him, assailing him with questions of what he saw. But he shook his head, thinking of the caterpillars writhing and squirming on the moist forest floor and said, "Nothing at all."

There Are No Skies, Only Depths

Deep beneath the oceans depths there slept a secret that had been forever kept. Of what it was no one was sure, but the ships and submarines that passed over its position were sent into disarray. Captain Hemlock sent two of his best deep-sea cruisers down into the darkness of the open oceans depths, but neither returned. He cursed in frustration, for the men he had sent to pilot the cruisers were his best, and now they were gone. A deep shame crawled its way under his skin, and he slept alone in his office that night. The next morning he awoke to the sound of alarms. The ship was locked in combat with something his sailors could only describe as a 'Sea Beast'. Captain Hemlock rushed to his station and began giving orders. He looked out of the observatory and had it not been for his immense discipline he would have gasped. The 'Sea Beast' the men had talked of was none other than the Kraken. Every child who grew up by the docks had heard the legends, although none of them believed them to be true. But now he was standing face to face with the beast, and as he studied its horrific body, its eyelids rolled back and a deep red eye glared at him. It was like the maw of hell itself, there was so much hatred in those eyes. How any living being could bare so much anger and hatred he could not explain, but he knew that the battle was a lost cause. Even his ship, the Paruse, a deep-sea artillery submarine, was no use against such a titan.

He ordered the men to abandon their stations, and he let go of the controls, lest the ship be torn apart in the struggle and they all drown.

With their surrender, the Kraken pulled the ship deeper into the darkness, so quickly that all on board felt the butterflies in their stomachs that come with vertigo.

This was the end, Captain Hemlock thought to himself as he clung to the handrails of the control deck.

Deeper and deeper they plummeted into the darkness, but suddenly the Kraken let go.

Captain Hemlock pulled himself up and rushed to the observatory, where he saw the tip of one of the Krakens great tentacles slip out of view of the ships lights and disappear into the darkness beyond.

The Paruse drifted within the darkness, its engines and propellers had been damaged beyond repair, and all that could be heard within the quiet deep was the attempts at distress signals from the crew. "We are the Paruse, deep sea cruiser 299, and we are lost at the bottom of the Great Sea. Can anybody hear us?"

The crew repeated this line over and over again, but static was their only response.

"We are on our own," Captain Hemlock announced stoically.

Days moved by and still the Paruse sank deeper and deeper, so great a distance that it was incomprehensible to the Captain Hemlock and the crew. But one day the crew saw light.

They rushed to the windows of the observatory excitedly and peered out of the glass where they saw a small blue orb of light floating beneath them in the distance.

They had no idea what it could be so deep in the oceans, and for a long time they simply stared at it silently, each member of the crew lost in deep thought.

Thirteen hours later they sank close enough to the orb of light that they could notice some of its details. Clumped on the surface of the orb were patches of green and light brown that rotated with the orb slowly.

This perplexed Captain Hemlock and his crew even further, for if not a creature of some sort, what else could exist so deep within the sea?

Still the Paruse sank closer and closer the orb each moment, until they were beside it, or what seemed to be beside it. They had not realised the enormity of the orb, for they were still what seemed an eternity away from it in distance, but it already dwarfed their ship, and as Captain Hemlock studied the surface of the orb he lost himself and gasped.

His crew surrounded him, never before had they seen their captain react in such a way.

"What is it, Captain?" asked First Mate Johnson, a look of concern on his face.

Captain Hemlock turned to Johnson and the rest of the crew and breathed, "It's Earth."

The Beginning of a Great Adventure

Beneath the soft warmth of the winters sun, the animals of the Great Forest went about their daily routines. The forest lay at the base of the Andule mountain ranges, whose peaks were blanketed in a thick layer of snow that glistened in the sunlight. The air was cold and heavy, but it was fresh, and as the soft breeze blew it carried with it the scent of tree sap.

If someone were to stand above one of the mountains and yell, their voice would echo powerfully over the forest. So tranquil and balanced were all the elements that worked there, that any sound other than the flow of rivers, or the rustling of trees, would disturb the delicate environment that flourished within the great forest. As the wolf pack ran they darted swiftly through the thick trees, chasing after some unlucky deer that had found itself caught in the middle of their hunt. These were not times of famine, but the wolves chased the deer as eagerly as they would have done so after weeks of starvation. Their manes were colourful and healthy, and as they darted and weaved their strong mechanical muscles pushed them on like well-oiled machines, fit perfectly for their use. The deer fell and the wolves closed in hungrily. This was just the natural order of things, for by the same force that the wolves used to consume they too would be consumed in the end.

Over the hillside, a steam train was rolling by, and as the black smoke billowed from its chimney it sounded its horn. The sound echoed through the forest, and the sensitive ears of the wolves and deer alike stiffened at the disturbance.

The train turned the mountainside and its passengers looked over the forest in awe.

"It's beautiful…" Miss Jane Morrowgood gasped.

She looked over to Jim Johnson, a fresh-faced but determined looking man. He nodded in agreement silently, staring off into the endless stretch of trees in the distance.

"I think that every time I pass this forest. I often wonder what life would be like as an animal in that forest, and a part of me knows it would be better."

"Better than what?" asked Jane, thoughtfully.

"Better than the life I live. A life of toil and back breaking work for the sake of other men," he replied.

His eyes were a strong blue, and as Jane looked at him she noticed the many scars and nicks that covered Jim's hands. And although she didn't realise it at the time, she was completely in love. So too was Jim, although he had known it from the first time he had ever met Jane's acquaintance. But they were from different walks of life, and the two of them knew deep down that their love could never be anything more than fanciful daydreams and thoughts.

"One day I will make a life in that forest," said Jim.

"Will I still be able to visit you?" Jane smiled.

Jim smiled back at her, "Always."

Nothing else was said, and for a time the pair stood and lost themselves in thought as they gazed out into the forest beyond.

That night when Jane had returned to her quarters from dinner she noticed a piece of parchment resting on her bedside table. She picked it up curiously and read the word "Always."

She gasped as realisation spread its way across her face and rushed out of her room towards Jim's. She flung the door open, the lights were off and his window was open, the curtain flapped gently in the cold night air. She rushed to the window and stuck her head out, the train was moving at a slow trot, and as she peered out into the distance she just made out footsteps in the snow not far behind. It wasn't too late. Jane hesitated for a moment, just a few months before she never would have dreamed of doing something so crazy, especially for a man that she knew her family would never permit her to love. But a moment after she shook her head, and without a second thought, she dove out of the window into the night, and ran after the footsteps in the snow.

Like an old man lost alone out to sea,
Or a dreamer lost at heart,
The moon is there in the darkness,
And from the darkness we all start

Happiness can never be a state of being,
It is merely a reaction,
The journey towards happiness becomes poison,
For we all get lost along the way,
Instead look for a purpose,
That gets you out of bed each day,
Happiness, sadness all you will face,
But with an undying purpose you will never stray,
From the balance that comes with being content,
With all of life's emotions,
Regardless of intent,
Good or bad all are real,
And your life will be full no matter how you deal,
Welcome pain and welcome love,
It's all a guessing game at the end of the day,
But I'd rather have a purpose than live to be the same,
Life's too short to just be happy.

Jealousy I know your name,
You swooped me up in your fatal game,
Until all that was pure and good was gone,
And cupid and his angels stopped singing their songs,
I stood there all alone in the silence,
With nothing but green jealousy and his violence,
And with his ugly head he turned and said,
"You're nothing compared to what's ahead",
I screamed at him and told him he was wrong,
But when I turned she was gone and he was right all along.

Disillusions

This was the land of eternal twilight,
And old stories of the suns awakening had drifted into legends that could hardly be believed,
We were not sad people, but some of us were lost within the darkness that swallowed our home,
And many people lost their hopes and dreams in the shadows that lay over our heads,
But I was not of age yet, and even the darkest of nights held the slight glow of beauty within their unknowing,
To a mind that has seen and thought much, darkness was a great nothingess, but a childs mind is empty save for the simple wonderment of being,
Every evening whilst the others slept I crept silently to the cliffside and peered out to the ocean beyond,

They say that across the horizons there are
lands washed with the warmth of the suns
light,
I didn't believe them until I started to look
closer,
And to my surprise I saw a ship far off in
the distance beckoning me to join it,
Its bright lights glowed like a beacon in the
darkness as it floated across the lonely black
sea,
and it drew me in like a moth,
 I lay awake and thought of it until it became
an obsession,
Until the day I decided to leave my home
and cross the dark waters alone,
Without a look back I hopped upon a
wooden row boat and paddled into the dark
sea until I vanished from view completely,
I paddled for hours on my small wooden
boat until I couldn't see land anymore,
But every time I looked back at the boat I
was no closer to its light,
I paddled faster, yearning to be aboard the
ship,
and too late I realised I never would,
I turned my wooden boat around and headed
back to shore,
And never again did I look out into the
horizon,
That was the day I came of age.

The Gorillas That Taught Man

We were hopelessly lost. It had been almost three days of walking blindly through the jungle, and on our search for civilisation we were often forced to huddle in fear of the roars and screeches that echoed around us. There were four of us. Me, Sir John Silva, Adam and Miss Maddison Blair. We were on our way to a conservationists' retreat that was meant to be held right in the heart of the jungle, but on our way, our driver suffered a heart attack and lost control of the car. The car veered off the road and we plummeted down deeper and deeper into the overgrowth before finally crashing at the bottom of a steep gully. Our transport was in a state of disrepair, and what was worse was that our driver, who was also our guide, was dead.

With little in the way of rations we set off at once to find the road again, but I fear in our confusion we started off in the wrong direction and it wasn't long before we became lost.

Sir John Silva lead the way, for at first glance he was the bravest and the surest of himself. I have always been an observer, even at school I preferred to sit out and watch the other kids play. From a young age, there was something that intrigued me about how people responded to the world around them, and it wasn't long before I saw through Sir John Silva's brave façade. For ease of the story I will henceforth refer to Sir John Silva as just John. Only a few hours passed before it was clear to me that John was as scared as the rest of us. I would have forgiven him for his delusions if they were for the sake of keeping us calm and together. But they were not. John loved the praise, he was a well-known chauvinist back home, and after he returned from the war he was never seen without his medals buttoned neatly on his chest.

I would have forgiven him for his egotism too, had it not been for his dogmatic reproachfulness to any ideas that did not come from him. I denounced silently that in his lead we were doomed. But, there was not much I could do. He was six feet four and just as broad, whereas I stood a mere five feet six, and constantly wheezed and coughed as we trekked.

I must admit that I was just as scared as everyone else, and I was glad not to lead, lest I too was to lead us to our demise.

But evidently, I was not the only one who was beginning to question John's methods. Miss Maddison Blair was hot on his heels, complaining at every step. It wasn't long before John reached his limit, and with a roar of frustration he told Maddison to shut her mouth. If I were a bigger man I would have fought for her honour right there, in the jungle, just the same as a Neolithic brute would have. But I was not.

John didn't stop there, he beat his fists against trees, he shouted and screamed, all while the rest of us stood watching in shock. We were lost, and hungry, and for one of us to break down was to be expected. What I did not expect was for something else to roar in response.

A roar unlike any other I have heard boomed from beyond the trees. All together we froze as we watched the tops of trees tumble before us, and a moment later, an enormous Silverback burst through the overgrowth. Hunched over on all fours he breathed heavily as his beady eyes darted between us. "Magnificent!" I said, as I gazed in wonderment at this extraordinary beast. It took my outburst as aggression, and beat its chest challengingly.

"Alfred bow your head!" Maddison warned me hurriedly. I did as she said, and the Silverback relaxed. It was more curious than scared. How could such a great specimen ever be fearful of man? And as I studied its body I wondered by what trickery humans climbed their way to the top of the food chain.

These creatures lived by the law of nature, and of dominance. We humans thrived from the laws of delusion and trickery. This was what set us apart.

Soon the Silverback was bored, and it turned around and made its way back through the trees. "We must follow it!" I said, looking eagerly at the others for nods of approval, but their faces were vacant. Were we not biologists?

John shook his head as he reached for his rifle, "This is not safe. This beast must be killed! Lest it changes its mind and decides to kill us."

"No John!" said Maddison, placing her hands gently onto his. John looked her and nodded.

But I was already racing ahead, I had travelled to the very heart of Africa to talk about the Gorillas, and here I was, just a few feet away from a Silverback!

The next moment I was trailing at the heels of the great specimen. It looked back at me uncaringly as I followed it, and I too looked back to see John, Maddison and Adam trailing behind me cautiously.

The Silverback disappeared into the trees ahead, and as we peered through I could not stop myself from gasping. We had been lead to an entire family of Gorillas! They were beautiful. There were females, children and younger males that play-fought and tried desperately to attract attention to themselves. It was as if I was looking into the very history of early humans. The others gasped too, and for a short while we all simply stood in amazement at the sight before us.

But suddenly an explosion rang behind my ears, and the great Silverback that had threatened us menacingly dropped to ground.

I looked behind me to find John holding up a smoking rifle.

"What have you done!" I said in disbelief.

"Saving us…" replied John, with a cruel smirk.

I couldn't believe it, and as the shot echoed into the distance the family of Gorillas rushed towards their fallen leader, wailing and beating their fists against trees.

And then their attention turned to us.

To be continued…

The day that the humans disappeared,
The water began to clear,
The day that the humans disappeared,
Only waterfalls and bird songs could hear,
The day that the humans disappeared,
We became one with the universe and its essence,
The day that the humans disappeared,
The world came back to life.

Forgiveness

The sun set over the valley and cast great shadows over the land. With the falling darkness, the noises of the forest grew silent, until all that could be heard was the occasional rustling of leaves or the beating of wings. The old man sat atop the mountain's peak and watched the sun fall beneath the horizon completely. Over his years of travel, he had made a habit out of watching the sun rise and fall daily. He believed in the great oneness of everything, and in rising and falling with the sun he felt more a part of the balance that encompassed all things on earth. He had lived in this forest for some time, his hair was long and matted, and his hands and fingernails were constantly caked in dirt. Many years before he was a lawyer in the city over the mountains, but his life had been cumbersome from the start, to say the least. And as his debt mounted and his wife began to turn his children against him he decided that modern society was no place for someone like him. He had always been an introvert, but he had never been lonely. All the same, most mornings he awoke from dreams of his family, and he often started his days watching the sun rise in silent reflection.

His face was set with wrinkles that came from too much thought and brooding. It was not an ugly face, but it was distinct.

He had thought of many things throughout his time in the forest, and every day he found more wonders hidden within the forest that lay beneath the mountains. He found waterfalls and fields full of butterflies that floated softly in the sunlight. He found deep caves that kept the creatures of the night safe and hidden from the bright sun. He found trees that were home to all manners of animals that he had never even known to exist before he had come to the forest. To him, the forest was the city of animals. The treetops were the highways and roads, and by the rivers able students practiced hunting and fishing under guidance of their teachers. The overgrowths were the concert halls, for all around birds sang songs in a language that the old man could not understand, but feel.

He knew that one day he would lay down with the setting sun, and never rise again with it in the morning. Many of us are fearful of that day, but to him, it was a day he looked forward to. That day he would be with the forest. He would rise with the sun and blow with the wind, he would be carried through the dense trees as the high notes of bird songs, he would flow with the rivers and teach the animals how to fish and hunt. He would join the great balance of things, and in its great beauty he would finally be forgiven.

Two people that were once in love now pass by without saying a word.

Precious Memories

Rain thrashed against the window as Old Whiskey sat down with a sigh. His two grandchildren Thomas and Buck had come to visit from downtown, and upon their arrival, their mother Natalie noticed a twinkle in her Father's eyes at the sight of his grandsons that she had never seen when she was growing up. He had grown softer with his age, and quieter too. It wasn't for nothing that he got the name Whiskey. Natalie remembered the nights where her father would stumble home from the pub, cursing other men unknown to her with slurry words and ugly faces. She was scared of him growing up, he was bull of a man that had always seemed so solid, but now she could barely recognise the old man before her that sighed in relief when he sank into his seat.

Natalie leant on the doorframe as Tommy and Buck ran over to hug Old Whiskey, and she smiled when they jumped into his lap.
Whiskey laughed and squeezed the pair of them, almost suffocating them between his arms and breast.
"My boys!" Whiskey exclaimed happily.
The rain was getting heavier, and as Whiskey and the boys talked and played Natalie went into the kitchen to make tea.
As she put the kettle on she listened to her father tell one of his stories to Thomas and Buck.
"Yep… when I was your age I was bombin' down hills on me skateboard with me mates! Almost died a coupla times too, but I won't tell you too much about that otherwise your mum would kill me!"
Thomas and Buck listened on eagerly, "Mum told us you saw a blue whale once."
Whiskey looked out of the window and recounted distant memories that felt as if they were from another lifetime altogether.
He nodded, "Yep, I almost rode him too! But he got away…"
The boys gasped. They were young and still believed everything that adults told them, and it wasn't an opportunity that Old Whisky was going to miss.
"Yep. I used to write letters to him. I called him Bluey, but me letters would always fall

apart in the water so he never got to read 'em!"

"You're lying!" Thomas giggled.

Old Whiskey smiled, "Never! One day I'll take you two boys to meet Bluey yourselves. Maybe you can take him some of me letters."

As the boys clapped excitedly Natalie returned with some tea for Whiskey and two boxes of apple juice for the boys.

Whiskey smiled at her when she handed him his cup.

"Thank you, Natalie," he said warmly and kissed her on the cheek.

For the rest of the day, Whiskey told the boys stories of when he was younger. Of the times when he would surf and skateboard all day in the sun with his friends. Or when they would explore caves and jungles and hide from animals that would chase them in the wild.

His stories would always end with him grabbing the boys and wrestling with them as they giggled, and Natalie laughed softly as she watched too.

As the day grew on the rain began to ease and Natalie looked at her watch.

"Sorry boys it's time for us to go, we have to go home and make dinner!"

Thomas and Buck gave Old Whiskey one last hug before they hopped off his lap and grabbed hold of Natalie's hands.

"See you soon, Dad," said Natalie as she led the boys out.

"See you soon, Natalie. I love you," Old Whiskey replied.

As Natalie and the boys left Old Whiskey sat silently in his chair and looked out of the window. The rain had stopped and thin pillars of light had begun to burst through the thinning clouds.

It was silent now, and as he leaned back on his chair he closed his eyes and smiled, remembering the days when he used to skateboard down hills with his friends.

The Best Problem

"Get that fuck'n plate in the oven, Danny," said Jake as he rang the service bell. It was lunchtime, and their little Café in the heart of South London was packed to the brim. It was a sunny summer's day and, outside around the common, there was a sea of people sprawled out beneath the sun, kicking balls, throwing Frisbees and sitting in circles passing around drinks. It wasn't often weather like this came around, and no one was going to miss the opportunity.

It was to Jake's joy and dismay that suddenly his little café had been maxed out with hungry patrons, and all of them were just as impatient as the next.

"Why the fuck would you wait in a forty-minute line just to complain about the food not comin' out quick enough?" asked Jake after one of the waitresses had passed on another complaint. He wiped the sweat from his brow and continued working. It was brutal work, there was no time to stop and think, and every time he and his team of exhausted cooks sent plates out, more tickets flooded in in their place.

After what seemed an eternity the rush finally slowed down, and the pace of the little café returned to normal.

"Fuck me," said Jake, laughing as he looked at his crew.

"I am thinking why I ever take this job…" laughed Danny, the Spanish cook.

"Because reading fuck'n Dostoyevsky or whoever you always ramble about couldn't make you any money, who's the idiot now, eh?"

Danny whipped his tea towel at Jake's arse, who jumped out of the way just in time.

The boys in the kitchen spent the rest of the afternoon cleaning and prepping for the next day, and it wasn't until James walked in that they stopped.

"Awight James?" asked Jake, as was customary.

James shook his head, "Nah, I'm fucked."

"What is wrong mate?" asked Danny.

It was unusual for the floor staff to become friends with cooks, for more often than not the two were arguing and blaming one another throughout the day, but the boys in the kitchen had grown to like James. James was used to working on building sites, so he was unfazed by the constant barrage of insults and banter that came from the kitchen and even dished it out himself.

"My shifts got cut and my rent's due at the end of the week," James replied, grimly.

Jake was not one for comforting people, but there was something in the bluntness of his words that gave encouragement.

"Mate, money problems are the best problems you could ever have. Scott over there, his mum's sick. I'd be fuck'n homeless if I had a choice between having money and my family. Fuck it mate, you lose it all and you make it back, just how it goes."

James understood, "Yeah man, you're right."

James clocked off and walked home. On his walk, he lost himself in thought. He hated working at the Café. He couldn't stand the customers, and the constant running around all day. It was dog's work. But there was something about the people that worked there that he had never encountered before. The people that worked in the Café were all dreamers. They were all on separate roads towards their dreams, and the Café had happened to be a crossroads for all of them on their journeys. There were students, musicians, writers and artists alike, who all slaved away at the Café. In the Café life at least felt like there was a purpose to his slave work, and at the end of it all, he would look back from success and smile at how far he had come. He had never felt that way on the building sites back home.

At the end of the week, James's rent was due, and he begrudgingly cleared his account handed it over with nothing more than twenty pence to his name. His flatmate looked at him nervously, "What are you gonna do man? At the rate you're going you won't have enough money to make next month's rent."

James thought of Jake and smiled, "Fuck it, man."

Don't Shit Where You Eat

I knew that I had never really been in love before I met her. I had been through heartbreaks, betrayals, and beautiful moments filled with the soft words of endearment. But I had never truly been in love. It's a cliché, but the moment I saw her I knew that she was of my kind. There was something about her that made sense to me, and when we were first introduced to one another at work we both knew we were thinking the same thing.

A few months passed, and every day our connection seemed to grow stronger, but I was hesitant to make a move. I knew deep down that it would work out, but I couldn't stand the thought of making my feelings known to her just to find out that she didn't have any feelings for me at all. Never shit where you eat, that's what my brother and his friends always used to tell me.

But one day I took a big steaming dump right on the dinner table. I asked her out for ice cream on our break, and to my relief, she agreed.

I waited outside for her to finish her shift, trying to keep it cool, but I was too excited to play the act. Instead, I paced around the block a couple of times, trying to rid myself of the giddiness.

Finally, her shift finished and I walked back to meet her as confidently as I could. As we walked beside one another it felt like we had been together for years. It felt so natural, walking next to her, and her presence made me feel like a man. She was so delicate and precious that I would have done anything to protect her. It was my role.

After we ate our ice-creams we walked towards the park outside of work.

We sat down and talked for hours. We laughed and made silly jokes, and the silences in between weren't awkward, instead, they seemed like silent affirmations of our connection. I gave my heart up wholly and unguarded to her, and as we sat and laughed and studied each other I had never felt so happy to be alive.

As the sun began to set people around us began packing up their picnics, but we stayed. Our conversation had turned to the topic of love itself. It was deep, and it revealed so much of her beauty to me.

The only problem was that eventually, I realised that she was in love with someone else.

I didn't go back to work after that.

Keys in The Desert

As the desert winds whipped sand over the land the camels groaned under the weight of Sir Henry's luggage. "Are you sure we're going the right way?" Miss Grey yelled over the strong gust.

Sir Henry did not answer, he was on a mission. They were in a terrible situation, and he knew it. He was thankful that Miss Grey did not understand the severity of their situation, lest she was to make things worse. He had regretted the day that he had ever set eyes on Miss Grey. Ever since the mutiny aboard the Argile and their exile she had caused him nothing but grief. They had been beaten in Oman, and chased with sticks and scythes over the border to Fujairah where they were placed in custody for days, all because of what Sir Henry called her loud mouth and pretty looks. If Sir Henry had never promised Miss Grey's Father, Lord George Grey that he would look after his daughter he would have thrown her on the first ship he could find. But their lives were not the only thing that was at stake. Lord George Grey had been framed for the murder of Prince Alfred, and it was up to them to save him from the gallows. They had been given three months to prove her father's innocence, and with only one clue to start their search they had boarded the first ship to Oman in search of a man called Jeffrey who was stationed in a little village on the coast called Shinas.

Alas, had they made it that far on the Argile their mission would have been over as quickly as it had started, but instead, they were hopelessly lost in the desert, following no path in particular and hoping that it would lead them to where they wanted to go.

Another day passed and the winds died down. It was on this day that Miss Grey spotted a small village half-buried by sand in the distance. "Look Henry!" she said excitedly. Henry glanced over and smiled when he saw the village in the distance, and his lips split from the dryness. "We're saved."

It took them almost an entire day to reach the little village, and upon their arrival, they were dismayed to find it in ruin. The village people eyed the pair distrustfully as they walked through the entrance, and it wasn't long before they were questioned by the local guards.

"What business do you come to Shinas for?" asked the guard. Henry's eyes lit excitedly, they had made it to Shinas!

"We come to visit Jeffery. Do you know him?" replied Henry.

The guard said something to his companion in Arabic and turned back to Henry and Miss Grey, "Jeffery is dead. He was found murdered in his house this morning."

Henry did not know what to say, Jeffery had been their only clue, and with him dead there was nowhere else for them to look.

"Do you mind if we take a look through his house?" asked Miss Grey.

Henry wheeled around on her, but to his surprise, the guard nodded respectfully. "The daughter of Lord Grey is always welcome in Shinas."

Miss Grey almost blushed as she curtsied, and shot Henry a dirty glance.

"Pardon me, but how do you know who I am?" Miss Grey asked the guards politely.

"Jeffrey and your father were heroes in this land. Your father often boasted of the beauty of his daughter, it was not hard for me to realise it was you."

Henry rolled his eyes as Miss Grey's cheeks turned a darker shade of scarlet.

After the pleasantries, the group made their way towards Jeffrey's house, which was located on the other side of the village.

"What happened here?" asked Henry as they walked.

The village looked as if it had fallen victim to an enormous storm, houses had collapsed and the ones that remained standing were in no better shape.

The guard spat, "We were raided last night."

"That's awful! By whom?" gasped Miss Grey.

"Fanatics. Some desert cultists that search for the Sacred Keys," replied the guard.

"The Sacred Keys?" asked Sir Henry.

The guard looked at Sir Henry and Miss Grey and replied quietly, "Some questions are better left unanswered."

Henry and Miss Grey shot each other quick glances.

They finally arrived at Jeffrey's house. It was a beautiful home, built from sandstone and palm it blended in with the desert oasis around it.

"The door is open, we will stand watch out here," said the guard.

Henry and Miss Grey nodded and entered.

It was dark and messy. Whoever had come to murder Jeffrey had also torn his house apart.

"They must have been looking for something…" said Henry as they climbed over the debris strewn across the floor.

"Check his coat pocket," said Henry, pointing to the coat hung by the door next to Miss Grey.

She rummaged through his pockets and pulled out a piece of folded parchment.

"It's a letter!" she said.

"What does it say?" asked Henry.

Miss Grey began to read aloud,

Jeffery,
Our plan has worked. The Lord has been imprisoned and sentenced to die, but had it not been for his associate Sir Henry and his daughter Miss Eliza Grey, he would have been sent to the gallows by now. The pair are aboard a ship and are on their way to Shinas as I am writing this. But have no fear, I have some men on that boat that will see to it that they never make it to Shinas. Our time is almost at its fruition brother.

Keep the key safe for my return,
The Shadow.

Miss Grey looked horrified, "Jeffrey was plotting against my father this whole time!" Sir Henry was troubled, "If he was working against your father, then why was he killed? Come, we're not safe here."

Miss Grey tucked the letter into her coat and the two left the house to find the guards lying dead in the sand.
They looked around hurriedly for any signs of the attackers, but only the open desert and the shifting sands were to be seen.

To be continued.

The honesty of falling asleep,
Nowhere left to run from thoughts,
Be aware of what you dream,
Lest your life be caught,
Buried in mounds of disappointment,
For there are no great destinies for you,
Only things that you create,
With rusty tools and super glue,
There is beauty in the nothingness,
A great oneness of being,
For without great struggle,
Happiness is not worth seeing.

To have arguments in your head,
With bosses, partners and friends,
Maybe you should speak your mind more.

Too polite for a confronting world,
Too chivalrous to get a girl,
Nice guys never score.

It's ok to be a bit of a dick,
You're probably over thinking it,
Assertiveness is something to explore.

The greats never gave a damn,
About anything but to expand,
What they knew they were alive for.

No one is in your way but you,
The road is only for you to choose,
A blank canvas for you to draw.

Fuck what they think,
The world is yours.

Silence Is the Sound of Life

In the days of old, before the time of music and instruments, all that could be heard were the sounds of nature. The sounds of flowing rivers echoed through the forest, and as the birds sang their voices were carried through the trees so that all around could hear and feel connected to the land around them. But one day, man heard the beautiful sounds that came from the land and devised a plan to replicate them for himself. Man had no place in the forest, and although he frequented it often, he never stayed longer than what it took to hunt for food.

But, for all his immaturities man did understand beauty. He understood the music that came from the swaying of trees in the wind, and the pure notes of chirping birds. He understood that there was art and grace within nature, so man brought out his axe and cut the trees down, twisting and manipulating its wood into hollow instruments they believed could replicate its sweet sounds. The soft notes of birdsongs woke the forest each morning, so man killed the birds, and stole from them their feathers. The deer that roamed the woods, clapped against the rocks with their hooves, and so man killed the deer and stole their hooves. Man did this for everything in the forest, and at the end of the massacre, the people returned to the shelter of their village just outside of the forest.

For weeks, they hid within their village, twisting and practicing the sounds that were created from instruments that had been stolen and carved from the forest.

The day came when the men and women of the band announced that they were ready to share their music with the world.

They boasted proudly to the village that they had never heard more beautiful sounds than what had come from their instruments and voices.

And as the band played they opened the village gates, and the people flooded into the forest beyond, believing themselves to have given the gift of music back to the deer, and the wolves and birds that called the tranquil forest their home.

But the beautiful music that man had thought he created was like hellish screams to the creatures of the forest.

The trumpets stifled out the sound of the rushing rivers, and the heavy drums beat rhythms through the once tranquil woods and awoke all that had been resting peacefully. So beautiful was the sound that man believed he had created.

And when the choir sang, they attempted to mimic the subtle notes of birdsongs, but all that came out were twisted high notes and ear-piecing screeches that they mistook for the voices of heavenly angels.

Man tried to replicate the sounds of rivers and swaying trees, but it was putrid to the fine-tuned ears of the wildness who heard it for what it was. Doom. The coming of the end.

The forest was never the same after the day the band played, and as the people returned to their village they celebrated, for had they not given the world the greatest gift of all?

And as they celebrated the band played louder, amongst yells and cheers of good fortune and health. Fireworks exploded in the sky, followed by the 'oo's' and 'ahh's' of the spectators that partied below.

If one was to listen to the great party from the forest it would sound like a great war full of cannon fire and shrieks.

And after the great celebration, the people lay drunk in the street, pleased with their music and the beauty that they had blessed the world with.

Soon silence became the sound of nature, for man had stolen everything else. There was nowhere else but the mountains you could find a place that stood in silent beauty. There was no need for sound in the mountains, for there is no sound as heavenly as silence. Silence. What was and what will be. What is and what isn't. Silence is the sound of life.

Honest Criminals

"Bullshit that ever happened you fuckin' liar!" laughed Mickey, refusing to believe another one of Football's outlandish stories. Football was beside himself, "Swear on me mum's life. There was seven of em', and all of em' wanted a piece of me!"
"A piece of you? You're fucking skin and bones bro!" Scotty replied.
"Aye watch it, Football's had more pussy than all of us, he's just paid for it all!" Mickey laughed.
"Fuck off dickheads! Craziest part was they got me to lay under a glass table 'nd then they all took turns takin' shits on it." Football finished.
Steven choked on his water, "That's fucked!"
"Yea…" Football admitted, "I was into it but…"
The boys laughed as they sat and ate by the mouth of the river.

They had been on the run for days, and it had become an unspoken custom to listen to Football's stories at every meal. None of the boys complained, they loved hearing them, and every story was just as outrageous as the last. There were four of them in total. Football, a forty-something ex-cabinet maker who had been to Thailand more times than he could remember, and after drinking and smoking every day for over twenty-five of his forty-odd years he looked about ready to keel over and die at any moment. There was Scotty, a young buck in good shape who grew up having dreams of playing professional rugby, but had a recurring knee injury that put an end to his dreams. Next was Mickey, a small-time drug dealer that got caught in the wrong place at the wrong time, and finally, there was Steve. Steve was a quiet guy, although his quietness didn't make him any weaker. He had the aura of a leader, and when he did say anything, it was well thought out and reasoned.

All these men came from completely different walks of life, the one thing in common they had was that they were all criminals. After injuring himself, Scotty went down a path of daily drinking and frequent brawling. He loved to fight, and it never took much for him to fire up, but one quality he had was that he never held a grudge. After a good fight, he'd shake hands and walk away happily. But one day he punched on with an undercover cop, and that was him done.

Mickey sold weed and pills so that he could buy a car to drive his daughter to school, the only problem was that he smoked most of his supply of weed, and gave a lot of his pills away to his friends for free. He was a local legend, but he was also as good as dead to the local suppliers. A couple of months into dealing he already owed eight grand, but before the big dogs could put a hand on him he was nabbed by the cops. It was a blessing in disguise.

Steve, on the other hand, had lived most of his life in a quiet country town on the outskirts of New South Wales. He worked on a farm and lived a mostly wholesome life. Before prison, he had a loving family and a steady income. But, one day he walked in on his wife and friend Darren in bed and he lost himself in a blind rage. He killed them both in cold blood.

Every night after that incident he lay awake in his cell, replaying the events in his head over and over again.

Football was just Football. No one knew what he had been in prison for, but they all agreed that he should have stayed in there.

Although they were all criminals, none of them were bad guys. They weren't good, that's for sure, but they were honest.

Until just a few days before the four of them had been strangers, besides Mickey and Steve, who had been cellmates.

The prison had been dodgy from the start, even to the standards of some of the hardest and roughest boys the state had to offer. It was so bad that one day it came to a tipping point, and after a guard purposely knocked an inmate out during mealtime a massive riot started. Chairs flew, inmates and guards wrestled with one another, and in the commotion ten inmates managed to break out.

Six of the ten were caught on the first day, but by nightfall the four boys managed to lose the guards in the state forest.

Every day they walked as far as they could, stopping only briefly to eat and drink what was left of the lunchtime supplies they managed to grab on the way out, and also to listen to Football. The first night after they escaped it had dawned on all four of them that they could never return to their old lives.

"When we get out of this forest, I'm gonna hitchhike as far north as I can get. Maybe I'll get a job on a banana farm or something," said Mickey as they walked.

"I'm probably just gonna lay low at my aunty's place for a while till it all blows over a bit. Got a mechanic mate who'll let me work for cash I reckon," said Scotty.

"Mechanic… Now that's a fuckin' criminal! I dunno what you cunts are on about I'm goin' straight to Thailand…" said Football, panting from the mornings walk.

"I'm gonna tell my daughter I love her, and that I'm sorry," said Steve quietly.

Nothing else was said for some time as they walked in silent reflection.

That night they sat around in the moonlight talking.

Steven was telling the story of how he and the rest of his workers got laid off one day a few years before he went to prison.

"Yeah… They brought in machines and laid everyone off. Heard the manager got a big pay rise out of it too. What makes me angry though is that he promised me if I signed the contract he'd make sure me and my boys would have work, but he fuckin' lied through his teeth."

"That guy's the real fuckin' criminal. All I did was punch someone in the head!" replied Scotty.

"Yeah… Every man has his price, I guess some men's prices are less than others," said Steven.

The next day they came upon a clearing in the forest where they saw a small town in the distance.

"Fuck me dead!" said Football happily.

They walked with an extra spring in their step towards the edge of the forest, but before they left Steve stopped them. "Let's all split up. Would look pretty sus' if we all came out together… We're probably all over the news."

The others agreed, and after a short and unceremonious goodbye they went their separate ways.

Not a week passed before all of them had been caught.

Football got caught trying to get a free root at a local brothel, he hadn't even jumped towns before he was inside the dollhouse again.

Mickey got caught on a train towards Coffs Harbour, he never made it to the banana farms.

Scotty got in a fight at a gas station while he was on the run, and was caught soon after.

Steve made it to his mother's house, where his daughter was living. He had just enough time to hug her and tell her that he loved her and that he was sorry. But after watching the news of his escape his mum knew that he would come, and she warned the police. A moment after a force of riot police broke

down the door and arrested Steve in front of his daughter.
And so, the journey ended right where it had started.

The King of The Isles

Angus's first shift at his very first job didn't go at all how he had planned. He had imagined his co-workers to be hardworking and supportive, the managers to be leaders and friends, and also, he expected to have funny work banter with his work friends throughout his shift. In reality, it couldn't have been further from his expectations. He arrived at a quarter to eight at night to start his first shift re-stocking the shelves at his local supermarket. His hair was gelled, his shirt was tucked, and his new black leather shoes were polished and cleaned. But the man who greeted him was anything but. His name was Quintin, and he was the Nightfill Captain.

He was middle aged and balding, his buttoned shirt hung out on one side of his pants, revealing a belly with a thick layer of greasy hair, and as he stuck his hand out Angus hesitated to shake it.

"What's up man, I'm Quintin," he said, and as he grinned Agnus saw the thick set bags that sat heavily under his eyes.

"Hi Quintin, I'm Angus. It's nice to meet you," Angus replied, trying his best to respond in the professional manner his school had taught him to use.

Quintin almost smirked as he eyed Angus up and down.

"Come on, I'll show ya round."

Angus followed Quintin through the isles where customers were still shopping, Angus smiled and greeted them but Quintin brushed them out of his way. "You ever had a job before man?" Quintin asked.

"No, this is my first one," replied Angus hesitantly. He half expected Quintin to turn around and fire him on the spot for lack of experience. But he didn't.

"That's all good man, it's not rocket science. Fuck, this place is way different to when I first started. That was like twenty years ago," Quintin began.

"Wow, that's a long time!" said Angus.

"Yeah bro. Back in the day, if you didn't like someone you'd just fight them in the cool room aye! Fuck, it's all different now,"

Quintin continued, reminiscing in memories that were long gone.

Angus didn't know what to say, he was shocked at the lack of professionalism he had witnessed, all the while they were still around the stores customers.

Quintin showed Angus the back rooms, the lunchroom, bin room and the freezers, and after demonstrating ironically how to take a packet of biscuits out of a box and place it on the correct shelf he set Angus to work.

Angus worked as hard and as fast as he could, even though Quintin wasn't the suited up professional he thought he would meet, he still wanted to make a good impression. By ten o'clock the supermarket had closed to customers, and the isles were flooded with more boxes to stack.

If Angus thought Quintin had been unprofessional earlier, he was unprepared for what was to come.

There was one person stacking per isle, and because of the separation, there was no chatter and no laughter, instead when co-workers crossed each other's paths, it was with an awkward smile and nothing more. The only thing that could be heard was the supermarket radio that played old classics like Sweet Caroline on repeat. Angus didn't mind the music at first, but after a few hours it became torturous.

After a long absence, Quintin finally re appeared. Angus had wondered what Quintin had been up to in the hours that had led up to that point, and he soon realised that it was fuck all.

Quintin had been asleep in his musky brick walled office in the back of the store the entire shift.

In fact, Quintin was always sleeping. Angus wondered if he ever got a good night's sleep when he wasn't at work. Sometimes Quintin would fall asleep standing, one time Quintin even fell asleep mid-sentence. Angus thought he was having a heart attack as he swayed back and forth with his eyes closed, but a moment after he resumed talking like nothing had even happened.

Quintin strolled around the supermarket singing at the top of his voice, or telling the same shitty joke to everyone in different isle, Angus could hear him making the rounds one day with a packet full of knives asking everyone, "Oi do you wanna be chopped, sliced or diced?" before laughing his head off.

Angus must have listened to him re tell that joke over four times, and it wasn't even funny. He dreaded the day when Quintin actually came up with a joke that made someone laugh.

Angus had always thought of Quintin as being the peak of ignorance. He hated what he was. He was a delusional, stupid slob, but he was king in the supermarket. Quintin had walked the same isles for twenty years. He was the biggest fish in the pond, although that pond was full of tadpoles that eventually grew legs and hopped out.

After a while Angus came to admire Quintin in a weird way. He had never seen someone so confident and happy with themselves, even though Quintin's appearance betrayed any of those conventional ideals.

One day the branch manager of the supermarket came and yelled at Quintin in front of everyone to make a point, but Quintin wasn't fazed at all. He walked past Angus afterwards and said, "I bow to no one aye…"

Angus laughed in agreement.

Angus was almost jealous of Quintin. There was nothing higher in Quintin's world than being the Nightfill Captain. He had ascertained what he saw to be the lead role in life at fifteen, and he was happy where he was. Not many people could say the same thing. Even Angus's father, who was a respected barrister, often came home in volatile moods full of self-loathing and alcohol abuse.

Quintin was the king of his world, and he reigned supreme in the supermarket during the hours of eight o'clock to one o'clock.

Angus never asked Quintin what he did outside of work, there was a part of him that didn't want to know, he had a feeling it would spoil the illusion.
Eventually Angus found another job, he was sick of the late hours at the supermarket.
And eventually he forgot about the bad hours, and the terrible music, the awkward smiles and the late nights with no sleep.
But he never forgot Quintin.

Looking through the window within,
Memories spin ethereal around you,
Music plays but you can't quite grasp the notes,
There's a storm outside but you feel safe,
And as the wind howls you look through old pictures and smile,
Your memories are safe inside,
You're floating away in the darkness,
But you feel at peace,
Those memories are for another time,
It's time to awake from your sleep.

The storm came and washed the world
away,
The thunder brought down the buildings,
And the lightning set fire to the streets,
The ocean swallowed the land,
Until all was covered by sea,
And all that was, perished in the storm,
Save for a single rose sitting on a crown of
thorns,
And when the land rose above the water
once again,
The single flower began to shed,
Tears of gold over the destruction that had
been caused,
For what was could never be anymore,
But then the world started anew,
Creatures of light stepped from without the
blue,
Of the great oceans where until then they
had slept,
And forevermore the world and its light was
kept,
Safe in the palms of the beings so pure,
And finally, the world come back to life.

Memories of Higher Times

"Bruz, pass me the doink!" said Jesse with his arm outstretched. It was a Friday night and he, Arlo and Rueben had all snuck out together to smoke down at the netball courts.

Arlo passed the joint to Jesse, holding his chest as he coughed out smoke, and the three of them burst into laughter.

"Do you reckon we'll still do this when we're older?" asked Reuben. He had always been the sentimental one.

"No fuckin' way dude, I'll be on a super yacht when I'm older travelling the world with fifty chicks by my side," Jesse replied as he exhaled.

"Yeah, I bet dude, right after I'm done boning your mum!" said Arlo.

They laughed as Arlo and Jesse play fought.

It was a still night, and as the boys finished off the joint they sat down and looked up at moon in silence.

"Fuck space is cool," said Arlo after some time.

"Yeah… So many stars and so many other planets. There's definitely gotta be life out there somewhere," Jesse replied.

"For sure dude, I was watching a documentary about the Aztecs and stuff, they literally had drawings of aliens on the wall," said Reuben.

"So cool man, have you guys watched Planet Earth with David Attenborough?" asked Arlo.

Both Reuben and Jesse replied in unison, "I fucking love David Attenborough!"

The conversation continued in loops for a few hours before the boys finally packed it in and went home.

They were simpler times, before the boys left school and had to get jobs. Although their twenties were much the same. But as the years passed they stopped smoking as much, and one weekend without knowing it they finished the last joint they would ever have together.

By their early thirties all three of them were married. They loved their lives, and their kids, but they'd often meet up and reminisce about the days when they used to get high at the netball courts.

A decade passed and the three of them met up after Arlo's son completed high school, they were having beers on Jesse's balcony when Reuben asked them if they wanted to smoke one last time.
Jesse burst into laughter, "Fuck no!"
For the rest of the night the three of them sat laughing together, talking about space and David Attenborough, until it got too late, and they had to go back home to their families.

What was and what will be,
Are very much the same,
What is and what isn't,
Cause entirely the same pain,
What could have happened and what did,
Make us feel shame,
Lost in memories what could we gain,
But feelings of sorrow that hurt the brain,
To live your life should be the total aim,
Forget about the passing rain,
For in the end all feel the sun,
Until it sets and the day is done,
And then we wake up again.

An ocean full of fears,
The tide pulls in the weary,
Rain drops mixed with tears,
That hide the pain of the teary,
Sunshine that soaks warmly,
In the bodies of those that feel alone,
For how could they be,
Within the world that we call home,
The sun, the sea and the highest mountains,
All exist for you,
The stars and the moon,
The greatest droughts and the wettest monsoons,
All exist within your soul,
The universe before us is what makes us whole.

Find Your Wings

"What is love?" the Caterpillar asked the
Mockingbird one afternoon atop the tree
they shared,
"Love is the wind against your face and the
open skies at your reach. Come I shall
show you," it replied and then flew away,
But the Caterpillar could not fly after it, for
it was landlocked without the wings the
Mockingbird had been blessed with,
And soon the Mockingbird had
disappeared completely leaving the
Caterpillar alone atop the tree,
As it peered up longingly at the open sky it
came to a conclusion,
"Love is selfish".
The next morning the Caterpillar met a
lone Ant who was making its way down
the tree with a crumb almost twice his size
hoisted on his back,
"What is love?" the Caterpillar asked it as
it passed by,
The Ant lifted its head, straining from the
burden of the crumb on its back and

replied,
"Love is duty, to work and protect the ones
you care about."
As it crawled off once more the Caterpillar
said to itself with a scoff,
"Love is tedious".
That very afternoon whilst the Caterpillar
was indulging itself on the many juicy
leaves its tree had to offer it spotted a
Squirrel banging an acorn against the trunk
of the tree,
The Caterpillar, curiously watching the
Squirrel work away at the acorn posed to it
the very same question,
"What is love?"
The squirrel looked up from its task, tilting
its head and said "Love is the thing that
lays hidden within something",
Finally, the acorn cracked open and the
Squirrel dashed away to feed its family,
As the Caterpillar watched the Squirrel
dart off it saw that although the acorn it
carried meant nothing to the Caterpillar, it
was the duty the Squirrel held as a means
of feeding and protecting its family,
The breaking of the acorn was tedious,
But what was inside meant the prosperity
for the ones it loved,
As the Caterpillar sat and watched it
whispered to itself,
"love is beautiful".

That night the Caterpillar wrapped itself up
in a tight cocoon,
For the day had been long and it needed
rest,
And the very next morning the most
beautiful of butterflies arose in its place,
With a single flap of its golden wings, it
took to the open skies where it let the
radiance of the sun wash over its new
body,
And as it floated away in the soft breeze it
looked down at the tree that had once been
its home and said,
"Love is freedom".

If a single soul is made by two,
Then what of you is really you?
Are you half and half,
Or something other,
You have your fathers voice,
And yet you laugh like your mother,
Or are you something else entirely?
Travelling within the guise of a mortal
body,
An immortal soul,
Or a messenger of God,
A truly divine being,
Or perhaps you're just a simple sod,
I suppose in the end it's really your choice,
In truth, it's the soul that gives the heart its
voice,
So be you a sailor, thief, doctor or
blacksmith,
Cook, baker, plumber, or village idiot,
In the end, all are made fools,
For in reality there is only one true rule,
The law that will forever make you, you,
So now go forth! for there is much to do,
But remember always that a single soul is
made by two.

When you look into the mirror,
What is it that you see,
Do you see yourself as who you are,
Or do you see all that you could be,
There are endless things that rest inside your
eyes,
But there's hardly enough time in our lives,
To explore all the intricacies that make up
you,
I feel that part is for someone else to do,
The day you meet another like you.

Illusions in The Sand

It had been four days since Smoke's plane had crashed in the desert. He had set off in search of civilization with only three litres of water and some light biscuits to give him sustenance. He wasn't scared, but he was worried. As he trekked in the searing heat he thought of his family in the western lands, of his mother and father, and of his girlfriend too. He wondered if word had come to them of his plane crash, he assumed that everyone thought him dead. It was a strange feeling, being dead. He had never had so much time to think, as he walked through the never-ending desert before him. And as the suns heat became too much, he saw visions of himself as a child, running and playing in the sand dunes ahead. He chased the illusion, and as he got closer it looked up and laughed, running further and further away from him the nearer he got.

He chased it for what seemed like hours, but there was no real way of knowing. He had lost track of time in the ceaseless heat and thirst that assailed him.

On the fifth day, he could hear his mother calling out to him with words of love and forgiveness.

He would have cried had the desert sun not already drunk up his tears.

On the sixth day, he wondered if his family and girlfriend had ever really existed. He wondered if the world around him actually existed outside of his consciousness. He wondered if perhaps he was the only one that existed at all.

On the seventh day the heavens opened, and the voices of its angels sung down to him.

He opened his arms and welcomed their calls, but they were muffled by the wind that blew and whipped the desert sand around him, and a few moment later a sand storm unlike any he had ever witness rose in the distance and blocked out the sky.

There was nowhere to run to, for the land around him was bare and empty.

And as the sandstorm raged before him he dropped to his knees and surrendered to the storm.

On the eighth day, he was found by two helicopter pilots lying unconscious in the sand. They rushed to his side, fearing the worst, but to their relief he was still alive.

They flew him to the nearest hospital where he was treated for severe dehydration and burns, and after a few days of recuperation he was able to leave.

The desert felt like it had all been a dream, but he knew that it had happened.

When he finally came home he was met by his girlfriend, who rushed over and planted a thousand kisses on his face. They laughed as they held each other in disbelief, for just a few days before both of them had been dead to one another.

Finally, he felt alive.

You Are Everywhere You Look

When I was twenty I met a group of travellers on the road up north. A couple weeks before I packed my car with a single bag of clothes and my surfboard, and without saying goodbye to anyone I started driving. I wasn't angry at anyone but myself. In truth, I was just a lost, anxious boy that was looking for answers anywhere but himself. I remember someone telling me once that everywhere you look you see yourself. I wasn't convinced. I figured maybe I needed to see the world to figure it out. I drove for almost a week before I pulled into a small town on the coast of Queensland. In Australia, every small-town kind of looks and feels the same, and even when you enter a new one you're greeted with a strange feeling that you'd been there all along, and had never really left.

I don't think I said a single word that week. I thought a lot. I remember pulling up to random beaches, just to sit out on my board for a couple of hours and stare off into the horizon. I love looking out into the horizon when I'm surfing. From the angle you're sitting at, it makes it look like the clouds are blending into the sea. I don't think I'll ever get bored of that. If I ever live to a hundred I'll still be staring at the sky and the ocean with just as much wonder. I guess those were the places that I found myself when I looked. Many more years would pass before I realised that.

When I finally stopped to sleep at the town's hostel I was exhausted. I'd been sleeping in my car on the highway, or in state forests up until that point. I didn't have much money, but by that stage, I figured fuck it, and I paid the twenty bucks for a good night's sleep and a shower.

The hostel was definitely what I paid for. A bed in a room that slept sixteen, and access to a communal shower that smelled of piss. I was expecting the hostel to be filled with loads of European backpackers just getting drunk and fucking everywhere. That's what my friends had told me when they went to Europe. My friend Slugger reckoned every chick in Europe wanted to have sex with him. I didn't believe him though, Slugger was literally the ugliest cunt I'd ever met. Maybe it was the accent. I wonder what foreign girls hear in it, I've always thought the Australian accent was super rough around the edges, I guess in a way it has a nice twang to it. But I had trouble imagining the elegant girls of Europe finding it attractive.

Instead of the drunk Europeans, the people in my room were all in their forties. They were on their way back to Sydney from a meditation retreat in the Daintree Rainforest. I had never met anyone that was into meditation before, and I've got to admit that when they mentioned it I had to stop my eyes from rolling.

But they were lovely people. They asked me where I was from, and where I was going. And when I told them they actually listened. They laughed, and smiled, grimaced and nodded at my stories, and showed general interest in everything I had to say. It's funny when someone does that to you, you end up returning the favour, and for the rest of the day I listened to their stories quietly, and of how they found their way to meditation and yoga.

That night we joined the rest of their meditation retreat by the bonfire on the sand in front of the hostel. There were around fifteen of them in total, and all of them were just as nice as the people in my room. It was a night full of laughter, love, and happiness. I felt myself beginning to open up to the world.

I loved it so much that I almost resented it in a weird way. It brought out the shy, goofy boy in me that I had tried so hard to bury. It was something in the way they looked at me that completely disarmed my defences. They valued me for who I was, even though I hadn't known them long. It was a weird connection, and it was even stranger so that they were years older than I was. Their love made me feel like loving myself. I think that's what scared me so much. My entire life I had felt undeserving of self-love. Not in a way that was harmful, or negative, but

I had never felt like I had done anything that was worth being loved, and to love myself without accomplishing anything was to me, the height of vanity. But these people just loved me simply for being me.
I didn't stay long, the next day I was on the road again, but I'll never forget that feeling.

News

Growing up I used to live next to an elderly couple called Bill and Julie. They were beautiful. Every day when I got home from school Bill would always try and spray me with his hose, or buy me cap guns to play with. And every weekend Julie would bake fresh cookies for my family. My little brothers loved them too, and as we grew older Bill and Julie almost became like a second set of parents to us.

Mum told me once that Bill and Julie had a daughter, but she lived far away and wasn't able to visit much. I asked them about her one day, but they didn't say much. There was a look of deep sadness on their faces that even as a young child I could understand, and I decided to never ask them about it again.

I found out later on that their daughter had run away from home when she was seventeen, and they hadn't heard from her since.

A few weeks after my fifteenth birthday, Dad got offered a new position as a branch manager right on the coast of Sydney. So, we had to pack up our things and move. It was a strange transitional period of my life, I remember walking through the house for the last time. Everything was so bare and empty, it stood like a hollow shell, dried out from the inside. As we pulled out of the driveway Bill was waiting for us outside with his hose, and he sprayed the car as we passed. We all laughed and waved goodbye, and as we drove further away Bill stood there watching us until we had disappeared into the horizon completely. I didn't mind the move, I made way more friends at my new school, and living by the beach had its perks. My parents gave me a surfboard for my birthday, and every day after school I'd go out into the water and practice on it.

Surfing became my life after that, and I'm thankful every day for it.

Years passed and my life had changed completely from when I used to live in the countryside next to Bill and Julie. I was out of school, legally an adult, and I jumped at the chance to move out of my parent's house and live with some friends in a small flat near the beach. I drove a shitty rust bucket around the area, we used to laugh about it.

It had no airbags and the brakes were almost shot. It's a miracle I never crashed it.

On Friday nights, the boys and I used to do donuts with it at the beach car park, I'll never forget the ear-piercing screeches that came from its brakes when you skidded out in it.

My friend Jenson used to hold onto the back of my car while he rode his skateboard, and I'd drive him up hills or around corners real fast. I remember that time so vividly, it's around the time when my Mum called me with some terrible news.

She was crying when I picked up the phone, and I immediately asked her what was wrong. She tried to tell me through sobs, but all I got from her was that Bill and Julie were driving to the supermarket, she was in no state to talk, and I guessed that the news must have been fresh. I called my Dad to make sense of it all.

I had never heard him talk so sadly. He told me that Bill and Julie never made it to the supermarket. Bill lost control of the car and crashed on the highway before the last turnoff and the collision killed them both instantly. I wonder if a part of them knew deep down that that morning would be their last. The thud of the car door closing was like the final nail in the coffin.

At least it was quick, is all I could say to myself when I heard the news. That news fucked me up for a couple of weeks. I would catch myself thinking about it while I was driving in my shitty rust bucket car, holding my breath every time I passed another car on a tight street. It's fucked how quickly your life can change.

I've got a lot of years ahead of me, but time just has a way of passing you by.

When I sit on top of the headland, I always seem to find myself staring down at the waves crashing below. They seem to move so slowly from that height, and if I hadn't almost drowned when I was younger I would have thought that that was their regular speed. Close up waves move so quickly, you'd have no chance of getting out of their way if one came towards you. When I was sixteen I paddled out into the biggest storm swell of the year. I was way in over my head, and pretty soon after I got out into the water my board snapped and I was sucked around the headland. The waves beat me around and sent me to the depths. I've never been so scared in my life. Just as waves move quick when you get too close, so does time. An hour seems so long when you wait for it. The minutes flick by one by one, and the seconds drawl on behind them. But if you were to look closer than seconds, even closer than milliseconds, numbers would fly by so quickly you wouldn't even be able to make them out. Looking at it like that makes it seem like there's not much time at all.

I hope there is. I've got a lot more living to do.

A Road to Nowhere

I remember the day I left my life behind, and as I walked away my mum was crying by the window. There comes a day when every mother's heart gets broken, but that's just how it goes I guess. I didn't really know where I was heading at the time, all I knew was that I needed change. I was in my early twenties, and every day I felt like I was wasting the prime years of my life at a job I didn't like, doing the same shit and thinking the same thoughts every day. All the old people I'd ever spoken to always gave the same warning, "Where the fuck did all the time go?"

I used to laugh at my friend Jimbo, he was thirty-five with a kid, and all he could ever talk about was sex. The irony was his missus never wanted it. Every time I got in the car with Jimbo he'd be eyeing girls up, and he'd even call out at them when we drove by. I never got why guys yell at girls from their cars. I guess it's the safety of being behind the wheel. Those same guys wouldn't dare say anything if they passed a girl on the street. Even if they did, I reckon they'd probably get rejected, I reckon they know that too.

Not Jimbo though, he was adamant every chick was after him. Even though he was a mostly happily married man, he'd eye fuck anything that moved.

I confronted him about it one day. I can't remember exactly how he justified it, but it was something like, "I'm just window-shopping man".

I guess Jimbo was trying to hold onto whatever feelings of youth he had left, the thrill of being young and chasing girls, and that's what scared me about my life. I was due to be Jimbo with just a blink of the eye. It was drizzling while I walked, and the flecks of rain occasionally hit my eye, so I'd rub them over and over again.

I'd been working on building sites for a few years by that point, and I had a bit of money saved up in case I got caught out and needed to get home somehow, so I wasn't really nervous about the road ahead, at least not at that time. I never planned to work on building sites, I'd always thought I'd get a job in the creative industry. The week after I finished school I enrolled at a university for a creative degree. I loved to read classic books, and I loved to write. I was entranced by the characters and the themes, and I loved to read about the authors. I loved writers like Jack London. That guy really lived it.

The writers back then really believed in something. That's what I loved about them. Their stories contained so many messages and thoughts that I never would have stumbled across if left to my own devices. But when I went to university, I realised that very few of the creative people I met there believed in anything but themselves. That's why I dropped out.

And even though I didn't have any qualifications to my name, I didn't regret it. I learned enough about the world from the boys on building sites, and I trusted what they said because it came from themselves. I went a lot of places on my travels. I jumped on trains, and I worked on boats too. I saw a lot of Australia, but eventually, my sights landed on Europe, so I bought a ticket to London and left the next day. That place really changed my life. There was so much going on. So many people from different places and all of them had great stories to tell.

I learned so much about people, and it felt good to realise that I was just a person too. I was on the road for four years before I finally came home. I remember the taxi ride to my mum's house. I thought she would be mad, but at that point, I didn't care, I just wanted to see her. When she opened the door, she burst into tears and threw herself into my arms.

She never asked me any questions about my journey, I don't think she wanted to know. She was just glad that I was back. The next week I got my old job back as a labourer and I went back to work. It felt good to have consistent work again, I'd forgotten how much I'd missed coming home tired from work and having a nap on the sofa. It's simple stuff like that you end up missing when you're away.

I thought that my life would be completely different when I returned, but nothing really changed, I guess it never really does. I was twenty-five, and I didn't know what was ahead of me, but I felt that it didn't really matter.

What I did know for certain was that I knew nothing, but at least after all the things I learned on the road I was happy knowing that I knew less than I did before I set out.

The End

Collections

E.H.

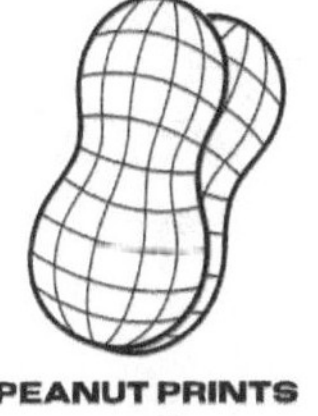

9 780648 546016